애경이의 꿈

Aekyung's Dream

글과 그림 ; 백 종민
번역; 백 종민

Written and Illustrated by Min Paek
Translated into Korean by Min Paek

CHILDREN'S BOOK PRESS • SAN FRANCISCO, CALIFORNIA

It was a beautiful and sunny fall morning. The sky through Aekyung's window was a clear blue. It was almost time for school, but Aekyung was still lying in bed, listening to the songs of the birds. She wanted to talk with them, but she was afraid to. "Their voices are lovely," she thought, "but are they singing in English or Korean?"

아름답고 햇볕이 좋은 가을 아침 이었읍니다. 창밖의 하늘은 맑게 푸르렀어요. 학교갈 시간이 거의 됐는데도 애경이는 잠자리에 누운채로 새들의 노래 소리를 듣고 있었읍니다. 새들과 함께 이야기를 하고 싶었지만 순간, 걱정이 되었어요. "참으로 고운 목소리아구나. 하지만 새들은 영어로 노래를 하는걸까 우리말로 노래를 하는걸까?" 애경이는 생각에 잠겼읍니다.

 Printed in Hong Kong through Interprint, San Francisco.
CIP data may be found on page 24.

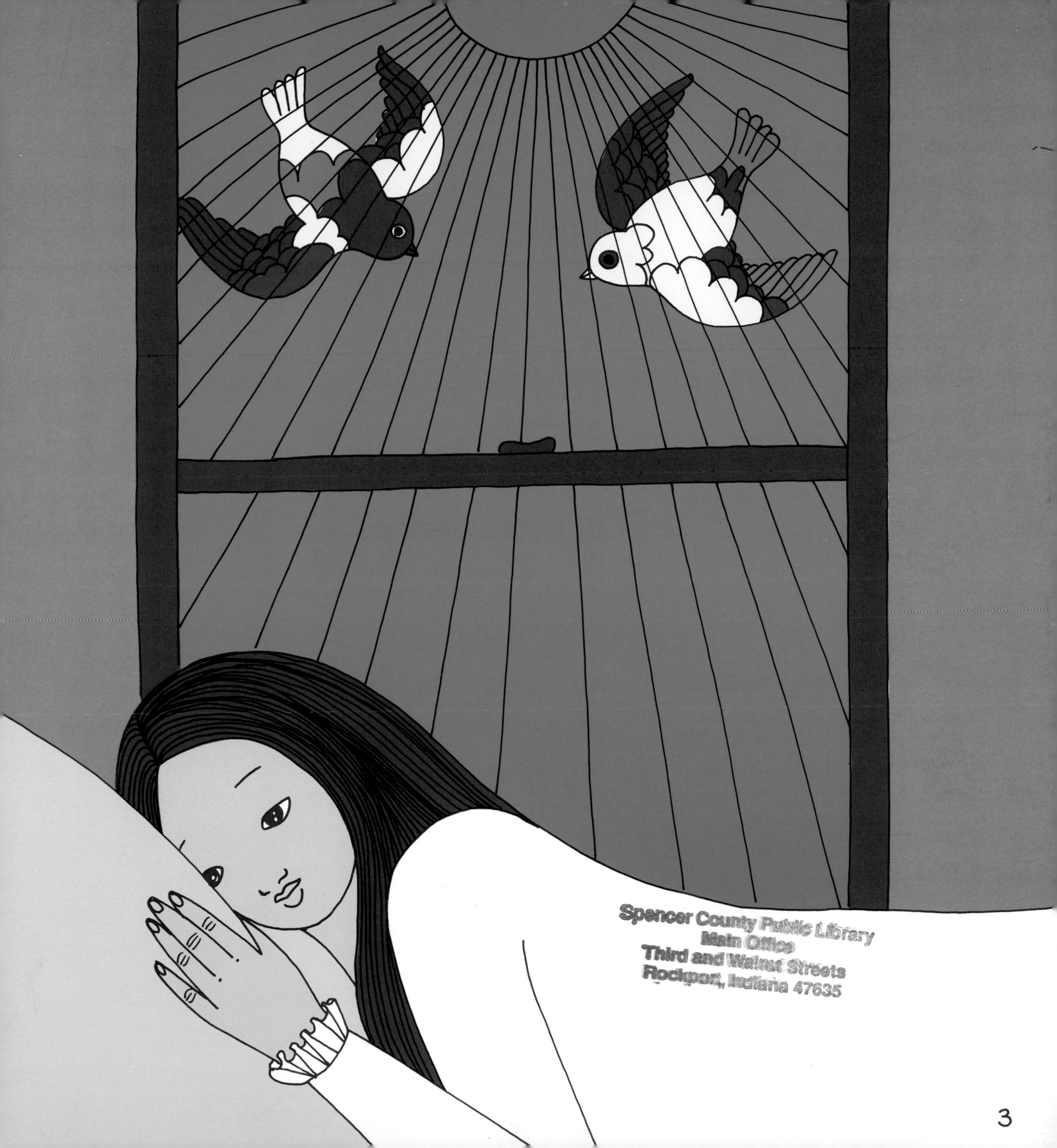

Aekyung felt terribly sad. She remembered how every morning in Korea she had jumped out of bed to open the window and say "Hello!" to the birds. But now she didn't even feel like getting up. "They must be singing in English," she decided at last. Aekyung had been in America for only six months and she didn't speak English very well.

애경이는 무척 슬펐어요. 한국에 있었을때는 날마다 아침에 일어나 창문을 열고 새들에게 "잘 잤니?" 하고 아침 인사를 했는데 이젠 일어나기 조차 싫어졌읍니다. "분명히 새들은 영어로 노래를 하는거야." 하고 애경이는 결정을 지었읍니다. 미국에 온지 육개월 밖에 안되는 애경이는 영어를 잘 할줄 몰랐어요.

"Get up, Aekyung!" called her mother busily from the kitchen. "It's a beautiful sunny day. You should get up and go to school!"

Aekyung didn't want to go to school. She was always alone there. Nobody ever played with her. The other day, one of her classmates had teased her about her "Chinese" eyes and then yelled at her, "Go home!" Aekyung had burst into tears. She was Korean, not Chinese. Didn't anybody know about Koreans?

"애경아 일어 나거라." 어머니가 부엌에서 바쁘게 부르셨읍니다. "오늘 날씨가 아주 좋구나. 어서 일어나 학교엘 가야지."

애경이는 학교에 가기가 싫었어요. 언제나 혼자 심심했고 아무도 같이 놀아주는 애들이 없었거든요. 전번날에는 한반애가 중국 사람눈을 가졌다고 애경이를 놀리며 "너희 나라로 꺼져라." 하고 큰 소리로 떠들어댔읍니다. 애경이는 왈칵 눈물이 나왔어요. 애경이는 중국 사람이 아니라 한국 사람이었거든요. 아무도 한국 사람들에 대해서 아는 사람이 없었을까요?

Aekyung tried not to say anything to her mother about what had happened. She knew how hard and late into the night her parents worked, and she didn't want to make them sad. But when her mother came into her room, Aekyung couldn't help saying in a trembling voice, "Mother, I don't want to go to school. I don't like to be teased for being different. Besides," she exclaimed, trying to hide her tears, "I'm Korean, not Chinese!"

"I know, my daughter, I know," mother replied soothingly. "But that isn't enough reason to stop going to school. You shouldn't let those mean feelings bother you. Just ignore them. Everything will be all right."

그날 놀림 받던일에 대해서 애경이는 어머니에게 아무말도 안하기로 했읍니다. 어머니와 아버지가 밤늦게까지 일하시며 고생을 하시는것을 잘 알고 있기 때문에 걱정을 끼쳐 드리고 싶지 않았기 때문입니다. 그러나 어머니가 방으로 들어 오셨을때 애경이는 떨리는 목소리로 말하지 않을수가 없었어요. "어머니 전 학교가기가 싫어요. 다른 애들이 제가 다르게 생겼다고 놀리는 것이 싫은걸요. 저는 한국 사람이에요. 중국 사람이 아니란 말이에요." 흐르는 눈물을 감추려하며 애경이는 말했읍니다.

"그래 다 안다. 하지만 그런것 때문에 학교를 안가면 쓰나. 속 상해 하지말고 그런 애들은 그냥 모른척 해버려요. 이제 괜찮아 질꺼야." 어머니는 애경이를 달래며 타이르셨읍니다.

Aekyung went to school the rest of the week and tried to ignore the teasing of the other children. On Sunday, Aekyung's Aunt Kim came to visit. She had just returned from Korea with many presents for the family and a fancy Korean dress for Aekyung.

"How was everything in Korea?" asked father.

그후 학교에 갔을때 애경이는 놀려대는 아이들을 모른척하려 애를 썼읍니다.
일요일, 김 아주머니 께서 오셨읍니다. 최근에 한국엘 다녀오신 아주머니는 많은 선물을 가지고 오셨는데 애경이에게는 예쁜 치마와 저고리를 선물로 주셨읍니다.

"그래 한국이 어땠어요?" 하고 아버지가 물으셨읍니다.

"Oh, it was quite different than when I was a girl," answered Aunt Kim. "When I arrived in Seoul, I couldn't find my old neighborhood. Instead of Kiwa houses, tall apartment buildings were everywhere. But the countryside is as calm and beautiful as ever, and the people care for each other as they always have."

Kiwa houses : traditional Korean houses

"아유 그렇게 달라졌을 수가 없어요." 하고 아주머니가 답하셨읍니다.
"서울에 닿고 보니까 좀처럼 제가 옛날에 살던 곳은 찾기가 힘들었어요. 기와집 대신에 높은 아파트 빌딩들이 꽉 들어섰더군요. 그러나 시골은 변함없이 조용하고 아름다왔어요. 그리고 인심도 여전히 후하더군요."

기와집 : 한국 고유의 집

Aunt Kim brought many color photographs from Korea. Among them, Aekyung recognized a picture of King Sejong of the Yi Dynasty.

"Do you remember what King Sejong did?" asked father.

"I haven't forgotten," replied Aekyung. "He created our Korean alphabet in the 15th century. Look, I can still write it." And she wrote down the 14 consonants and 10 vowels of the Korean alphabet.

"Very good," commented Aunt Kim. "Are you going to learn English as well as you know Korean?"

"I'm trying," she sighed. "But it's very difficult." Father looked at Aekyung and smiled.

김 아주머니가 한국에서 찍어 가지고 온 사진을 보고 있노라니 세종대왕님의 사진이 보였읍니다.

"세종대왕님이 무슨 일을 하셨는지 생각이 나니?" 아버지가 물으셨읍니다.

"기억하고 말고요. 15세기에 한글을 창조 하셨지않아요? 보세요. 아직도 잘 쓸 수 있는걸요."
애경이는 한글의 14자음과 10모음을 썼읍니다.

"장한데," 하고 김 아주머니가 칭찬을 하셨읍니다. "그런데 한글을 그렇게 잘 아는것 처럼 영어도 잘 배우겠니?"
"어렵지만 열심히 노력하는 중이에요." 애경이는 한숨 섞인 목소리로 답했읍니다.
아버지가 애경이를 바라 보시며 빙그레 웃으셨읍니다.

That night, Aekyung dreamt about King Sejong. She dreamed that she was back in his palace in the 15th century, and that he spoke to her:

"My dear child, you must be strong like a tree with deep roots. In this way, the cruel winds will not shake you, and your life will blossom like the mukung flower."

The court dancers pressed around her, offering her flowers. Then she woke up.

그날밤 애경이는 옛날 15 세기의 궁궐에 계시는 세종대왕님의 꿈을 꾸었읍니다. 세종대왕님이 애경에게 말씀 하시기를 :

"착한 애야. 뿌리깊은 나무같이 강해야 하느니라. 그래야만 모진 바람이 불어와도 넘어지지 않고 너의 앞날이 무궁화꽃 처럼 활짝 피어 나리라." 하셨읍니다.

궁중 무희들이 애경이를 둘러싸며 한아름의 꽃들을 애경이에게 주었을때 꿈이 깨었읍니다.

Mukung flower: Korean national flower

King Sejong remained in Aekyung's memory. As time passed, Aekyung stopped crying at home and in school. Instead, she spent her time repeating words and sentences in English. Soon, she was able to speak to her classmates in her new language.

세종대왕님의 꿈은 애경이의 기억속에 오래오래 남겨진채 간직 되었어요. 그후 애경이는 학교에서나 집에서나 울지 않았읍니다. 우는 대신에 영어 단어와 귀절을 반복, 연습 했어요. 얼마있지 않아서 애경이는 한반 애들과 영어로 말을 할 수 있게 되었읍니다.

One day in art class, she began to paint King Sejong in the royal palace. As she worked, some of the other children gathered around her. Among them was one of the boys who had teased her.

"Hey Chinese, what's that you're painting?" he asked.

"I'm Korean," answered Aekyung shyly, "and this is our great King Sejong."

The boy looked closer. "You sure are a good painter," he said. "You're a good Korean painter."

Aekyung beamed.

어느날 미술시간에 애경이는 궁궐에 계시는 세종대왕님을 그리기 시작했읍니다. 그러자 반 애들이 애경이의 주위로 다가왔읍니다. 그 중에는 애경이를 놀리던 애도 있었어요.

"얘 중국애야. 너 무엇을 그리는 중이니?" 하고 그 애가 물었읍니다.

"나는 한국 사람이야. 그리고 이건 위대하신 세종대왕님 이시다." 애경이가 수줍어하며 답했읍니다.

그 애는 더 가까이 와서 그림을 보더니 "너 참 그림을 잘 그리는구나. 그림을 잘 그리는 한국 사람인데." 하고 말했읍니다. 애경이는 기뻐서 환히 미소를 띄웠읍니다.

After school that day, Aekyung sat contentedly in her room, wondering how she could help other newcomers to America. The sun shone through her open window, pleasantly warming her black silky hair. She listened quietly to the singing birds... in English... then Korean... then, in English and Korean!

For the first time she realized that the birds understood the languages of all people. She looked out at them happily. "Hello!" she greeted them. "Hello! 안녕! Hello!" 안녕!

그날 학교가 끝난뒤 집으로 와 애경이는 기쁜 마음으로 어떻게하면 미국에 새로오는 친구들을 도울 수 있을까를 이리저리 생각해보았읍니다. 햇빛이 열려진 창문으로 가득히 들어와 환히 애경이의 검고 부드러운 머리결을 비추었읍니다. 애경이는 가만히 새들의 노래 소리를 들었읍니다. 새들의 노래 소리가 영어로 .... 우리말로 .... 영어로 .... 우리말로 하는것 처럼 들렸읍니다.

그때 처음으로 애경이는 새들이 이세상 모든 사람들의 말을 이해 한다는 사실을 깨달았읍니다. 어찌나 기쁘던지 애경이는 창 밖의 새들을 향해 "안녕!" "Hello!" "잘 있었니!" 하며 새들을 반겼읍니다.

:on·yúng (Hello)

About the Story & the Author / Illustrator

Since the repeal of restrictive immigration laws in 1965, there has been a tremendous influx of Koreans into the United States. Aekyung's Dream, a story about a recently arrived young Korean girl, centers upon an experience shared by all immigrant children ~~ that of adjustment to an unfamiliar, sometimes hostile, and oftentimes bewildering culture.

Ms. Paek's story portrays the psychological aspects of Aekyung's struggle for an ethnic identity in the mainstream society. Inspired by a dream about King Sejong of the 15th century Yi Dynasty, Aekyung begins to learn English and make friends at her new school. As her talents and individuality are recognized and affirmed by her peers, she once again becomes the confident person she had been before leaving her homeland.

Min Paek was born in Seoul, Korea, in 1950 and immigrated to the United States in 1973. Encouraged by her mother to begin drawing and painting at an early age, she has worked as a professional artist both in Korea and the United States. At the present time she is also a family counselor at the Korean Community Service Center in San Francisco.

In researching material for this story, Ms. Paek has drawn upon her many interviews with newcomers, as well as her own memories of her first months in this country. Aekyung's Dream was written with the hope that it might encourage other immigrant children to persevere in their efforts to adjust to a new culture.

Brett Chun, Staff Counselor
Korean Community Service Center
San Francisco, California

Series Editor: Harriet Rohmer
English Lettering: Roger I Reyes
Korean Calligraphy: Min Paek
Book Design: Harriet Rohmer, Robin Cherin, Roger I Reyes
Production: Robin Cherin
Editorial Assistance: Brett Chun, Betty Berenson, Tom Kim, *Director, Korean Community Service Center.*

Library of Congress Cataloging-in-Publication Data
Paek, Min
Aekyung's dream.
English and Korean.
Summary: A young Korean immigrant learns to adjust to her new life in America by heeding the words of an ancient Korean king.
[1. Korean Americans—Fiction. 2. Korean language materials—Bilingual] I. Title. II. Title: Aegyŏng ŭi kkum.
PZ50.531.P264 1988 [Fic] 88-18928
ISBN 0-89239-042-5